STONE A

a capsto

I Could Be a One-Man Relay

by **Scott Nickel**
illustrated by **Jorge Santillan**

STONE ARCH BOOKS
a capstone imprint

VICTORY SCHOOL SUPERSTARS

Sports Illustrated KIDS *I Could Be a One-Man Relay*
is published by Stone Arch Books — A Capstone Imprint
1710 Roe Crest Drive
North Mankato, MN 56003
www.capstonepub.com

Art Director: Bob Lentz
Graphic Designer: Hilary Wacholz
Production Specialist: Michelle Biedscheid

Timeline photo credits: Library of Congress (top left &
top right); Sports Illustrated/Bill Frakes (bottom); Heinz
Kluetmeier (middle right); Mark Kauffman (middle left).

Printed in the United States of America in Stevens Point,
Wisconsin.
102011
006404WZS12

Library of Congress Cataloging-in-Publication Data
Nickel, Scott.
 I could be a one-man relay / by Scott Nickel; illustrated by Jorge H. Santillan.
  p. cm. — (Sports illustrated kids. Victory School superstars)
 Summary: Since Danny has super speed, he is overconfident in his running
ability—will he learn in time that relay racing is about teamwork as well as
speed?
 ISBN 978-1-4342-2246-6 (library binding)
 ISBN 978-1-4342-3867-2 (pbk.)
 1. Relay racing—Juvenile fiction. 2. Running races—Juvenile fiction. 3.
Teamwork (Sports)—Juvenile fiction. 4. Sportsmanship—Juvenile fiction. [1.
Racing—Fiction. 2. Teamwork (Sports)—Fiction. 3. Sportsmanship—Fiction.]
I. Santillan, Jorge, ill. II. Title. III. Series: Sports Illustrated kids. Victory School
superstars.

PZ7.N557Iag 2012
[Fic]—dc2   2011033772

TABLE of CONTENTS

CHAPTER 1
Super Running.   6

CHAPTER 2
Dinner Talk   14

CHAPTER 3
Team Danny?   18

CHAPTER 4
Race Day.   34

CHAPTER 5
A Better Exchange   42

DANNY GOHL

Track

AGE: 10
GRADE: 4
SUPER SPORTS ABILITY: Super speed

CARMEN

TYLER

ALICIA

KENZIE

JOSH

VICTORY SCHOOL MAP

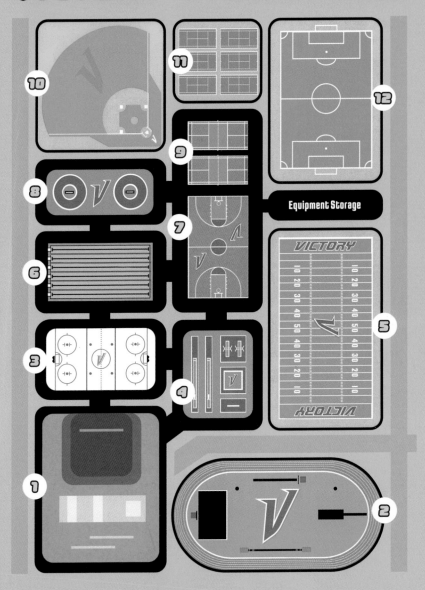

Equipment Storage

VICTORY

1. BMX/Skateboarding
2. Track and Field
3. Hockey/Figure Skating
4. Gymnastics
5. Football
6. Swimming
7. Basketball
8. Wrestling
9. Volleyball
10. Baseball/Softball
11. Tennis
12. Soccer

Super Running

On your mark . . . get set . . . GO!

I push off and my legs start pumping. They carry me down the track. I'm sprinting against four other guys, but I pull past them with no problem. Why wouldn't I?

When I'm not running track, I'm the running back for the Victory High Superstars football team. That means it's my job to be the fastest player on the field. And with my super speed, it's an easy job!

I finish the lap and slow down to a trot. I'm not even breathing hard.

"Did you see me, Coach?" I ask our track coach. "Did you see me?"

"Yes, I saw you, Danny," Coach Bolt says. "Nice job."

"I was the fastest — as usual!" I say with a smile. I'm glad Coach asked me to be on the relay team. With my fast feet, there's no way we can lose.

"Yes, Danny. Your speed is great for the team, but—" Coach starts.

Uh-oh. I sense a lecture coming. Think fast, Danny!

"Maybe I should do another lap!" I wave at Coach and pick up speed.

Coach Bolt is great, but I think he worries too much. Running is my thing.

That's why I'm at Victory School for Super Athletes. I don't need any help when it comes to speed.

Coach stops me before I get too far. "Okay, guys," he says. "That's it for today. Good start on the sprints. Tomorrow we work on timing drills. Practice is at 3:30, sharp!"

Adam, one of my teammates, groans. "Timing drills," he says. "Those are a killer."

"Yeah," says Shawn, another teammate. "You have to learn to time the baton pass just right. You have to pass it smoothly at full speed. It's tricky."

I shrug. "With Danny Gohl on the team, I don't think we need to worry about that," I say.

I grin and break into a sprint. In what seems like seconds, I am in the locker room, changing.

CHAPTER 2

Dinner Talk

At the dinner table that night, I'm feeling pretty good. I scarf down two pieces of my mom's famous roasted chicken. I even eat my veggies without being told.

"No fight over broccoli? This has to be a first," Mom says. "Someone must have had a good day at school."

"Really good," I say. "I totally aced the sprints. Beat the other guys like they were standing still. We start drills tomorrow. I can't wait for the first race. I'm the anchor. With my speed, nobody can touch us!"

"Too bad you can't make more of yourself and run the race alone," my twin, Alicia, says.

"Ha, ha, ha. Very funny, Sis," I say, but it isn't funny at all. "Can I help it if I'm the best?"

"Plus, you have the biggest head," Alicia adds, rolling her eyes.

"Mom!" I exclaim.

"Okay, you two. More eating and less talking," Dad says.

Mom points at Alicia's plate. "And don't forget that broccoli, young lady."

"See?" I say. "I'm even the best at eating dinner!"

Team
Danny?

The next day at practice, Coach goes over the basics. He tells us that the exchange zones are the areas of the track where runners can legally pass the baton from one runner to the next.

If we don't exchange within that area, we will be disqualified. It would be an automatic loss.

"The 4 x 100 relay isn't just about speed," Coach explains. "It's about strategy and teamwork. A team with four okay sprinters can out-race a team with four better sprinters. Do you know how? By beating the faster team in the exchange zones."

Adam, Shawn, and Harry turn and look at me.

Coach smiles. "But having a really fast anchor doesn't hurt," he adds.

I'm beaming. "Don't worry," I say. "Team Danny won't let you down."

"Team Danny?" Coach raises an eyebrow. He doesn't look happy.

"Yeah," I reply proudly. "I could be a one-man relay. I'm as fast as four runners combined!" I start running in place, my legs moving up and down.

The guys laugh and shake their heads.

"Okay, okay," Coach says, "enough showing off. Is 'Team Danny' ready to work on passing?"

We line up in our lanes. Adam is first, Shawn is second, Harry is third, and I'm fourth — the anchor.

Adam will pass to Shawn, who'll pass to Harry. He will pass to me, and then I take it to the finish line.

"Remember, guys," Coach yells. "The goal is to spend no more than 2.2 seconds in each exchange zone."

We start the timing drill. We'll be making the exchanges at full speed — running fifty meters each. I can feel my heart pounding in my ears.

As Adam sprints, Shawn gets ready for the exchange. Shawn takes off and reaches back for the baton. Then he exchanges with Harry.

It's my turn next. I'm eager to get the baton. Harry hits the exchange zone and I take off, reaching my hand back. It takes an extra second for Harry to reach me. When I get the baton, I speed up, running the final fifty meters easily.

I'm not happy. "Come on, guys!" I
shout. "You're too slow!"

"Take it easy, Danny," Coach says. "The
exchanges took a little longer than I'd like,
but we can work on that. It was a good
team effort."

I don't think Coach understands. It's not the exchange timing. It's the guys. They're not as fast as I am.

We run a few more, but it's the same problem. The exchanges aren't bad, but Adam, Shawn, and Harry just can't match my speed.

After practice ends, I hang around the
locker room until the other guys leave.
Coach Bolt is packing up some gear in
his bag.

"Coach, do you have a minute?" I ask.

"Sure, Danny," he says. "Is this about
the relay team?"

"Yes," I reply, feeling nervous. "I don't
know how to say this, Coach. I really like
them, but . . . I think the other guys are
holding us back."

Coach frowns. "Holding *us* back?" he asks. "Or holding *you* back?"

My face is hot, and I feel a little shaky. "Coach, everyone knows I'm the fastest runner! But just because I have super speed, I can't be expected to carry those guys."

Coach frowns again. "Danny, remember what I said earlier about strategy and teamwork? For a relay race, speed is great, especially super speed. But it's not as important as working together."

Finally, Coach smiles, so I know he's not that mad at me. "Why don't you sleep on it, okay?"

"Okay," I say. If Coach isn't going to listen, I guess I'll just have to depend on myself.

Race Day

Fast-forward a week. It's the day of the big track meet. I'm usually a little nervous before a game or a race, but for some reason, today I'm perfectly calm.

I have nothing to worry about with my speed. I know that even if the other guys mess up, I can pull out a big win for the Victory School Superstars.

Before the race, Coach Bolt gives us his usual pep talk. "We've drilled hard this week," he says. "Remember to run as a team, and you'll all do fine."

"Go, Victory!" we shout in unison.

Coach stops me as we're heading out to the track. He looks me in the eyes. "Remember, Danny. Teamwork."

I nod my head and look away. Teamwork, teamwork, teamwork. That's all Coach ever says. What about being a star player? Everyone loves a star.

There's a big crowd for the race, and I can see that the stands are full.

I decide I'm going to show everyone — the guys on my team, my friends, my family, and especially Coach Bolt — what I can do.

The race begins. It's just like we practiced. Adam's first. As he sprints, Shawn gets ready for the exchange.

Shawn takes off and reaches back for the baton. Then he exchanges with Harry.

It's my turn next. I'm ready. I see Harry getting closer and start running. I reach back and feel the tip of the baton. I close my fingers around it and speed up, pushing as hard as I can. In a blur, I finish my 100 meters. *Yes!*

Then I realize something's not right. I look down at my hands. They're empty. Oh, no! What did I do? I feel a knot in my stomach as Coach waves me over.

"Danny, you missed the exchange," Coach says. "That's an automatic disqualification."

I feel like a balloon that someone just let all the air out of. So much for being the star.

CHAPTER 5

A Better Exchange

The Victory School track team goes to Ron's Pizza Palace after every meet. Coach buys the team a large cheese pizza and a couple pitchers of root beer. It's something everyone looks forward to.

Usually I do, too . . . but not today. After being disqualified, I don't feel much like a pizza party.

Harry whispers something to Coach.
Coach smiles and makes a quick call on
his cell phone. I wonder if he's calling my
replacement.

I walk to the locker room alone and
change out of my uniform. *Ugh!* I just want
to go home and forget all about racing.

Soon, I'm sitting in my room. I am trying my best not to think about how I messed up when Mom calls to me. "Danny," she says. "You've got company. Hurry up!"

"What?" I groan. Can't a guy sulk in peace? I walk into the living room and see Coach, Adam, Harry, and Shawn. Coach is holding a big white box.

"Surprise!" Harry shouts.

Surprise? What surprise? Coach opens the box. Inside is a cake with an anchor drawn in frosting and the words "Team Danny."

"The guys wanted to do something special for you," Coach says. "They all chipped in."

I can't believe it. "But I let everyone down. I got us disqualified. Why did you guys do something so cool for me?"

"Duh! Because we're teammates," Adam says. "And we knew how important the race was to you."

"Everyone makes mistakes," Shawn adds. "But a team sticks together, no matter what."

Mom brings out plates and cuts each of us a big piece of cake.

Harry smiles. "Danny, we can work on that exchange some more during the next drills, if you want," he says. Then he grabs a fork off the table and holds it toward me.

I don't wait for a second. I snatch the fork in one, smooth motion.

"Hey," I say, grinning, "looks like my exchange is getting better already!"

GLOSSARY

anchor (ANG-kur)—the member of a relay team that runs last

automatic (aw-tuh-MAT-ik)—done immediately without discussion or thought

baton (buh-TON)—a short stick passed from one runner to another in a relay race

disqualified (diss-KWOL-uh-fied)—stopped from competing because a rule has been broken

exchange zone (eks-CHAYNJ ZOHN)—the area on a track where relay members can pass the baton

legally (LEE-guh-lee)—allowed according to the rules

relay (REE-lay)—a team race in which members of the team take turns running and passing a baton from one runner to the next

sprinting (SPRINT-ing)—running fast for a short distance

strategy (STRAT-uh-jee)—a clever plan for winning a race

ABOUT THE AUTHOR

SCOTT NICKEL

Scott Nickel works at Paws, inc., Jim Davis's famous Garfield studio. He has written dozens of children's books, including *Jimmy Sniffles vs The Mummy, Secret of the Summer School Zombies,* and *Wind Power Whiz Kid.* He is also the author *It's a Wrestling Mat, Not a Dance Floor* and *Skiing Has Its Ups and Downs* from the Victory School Superstars series. Scott lives in Indiana with his wife, two sons, six cats, and several sea monkeys.

ABOUT THE ILLUSTRATOR

JORGE SANTILLAN

Jorge Santillan got his start illustrating in the children's sections of local newspapers. He opened his own illustration studio in 2005. His creative team specializes in books, comics, and children's magazines. Jorge lives in Mendoza, Argentina, with his wife, Bety; son, Luca; and their four dogs, Fito, Caro, Angie, and Sammy.

TRACK IN HISTORY

776 B.C. The ancient Olympic Games begin with one event: a short sprint of about 600 feet.

1896 A.D. Sprint races and a marathon are part of the first modern Olympic Games in Athens, Greece.

1912 The American men win their first Olympic relay event, the 4 x 400.

1936 Jesse Owens becomes the first American to win four gold medals in a single Olympics. He wins the 100- and 200-meter races, the 4 x 100-meter relay, and the long jump.

1954 Roger Bannister of Great Britain becomes the first runner to complete a mile in less than four minutes.

1968 American Jim Hines is the first to run the 100-meter in less than ten seconds.

1996 American Michael Johnson is the first Olympic sprinter to win gold in the 200 and 400 in the same year.

2009 Jamaican sprinter Usain Bolt breaks his own record for the 100-meter dash, running it in just 9.58 seconds.

Danny Gohl Is Speeding Toward Victory!

If you liked reading Danny's adventure in track, check out his other sports stories.

A Running Back Can't Always Rush

With his super speed, Danny can rush down the field in seconds. But when he forgets to slow down off the field, he faces big problems. How will Danny learn that a running back can't always rush?

It's a Wrestling Mat, Not a Dance Floor

With football season over, Danny tries wrestling. When he uses his super speed in his new sport, he ends up dancing all around. Danny's got to remember that it's a wrestling mat, not a dance floor.

Skiing Has Its Ups and Downs

Danny expected to be the best skier at Triumph Mountain. But he was wrong. When he goes too fast, he falls. When he's extra careful, he's too slow to win. Danny is ready to quit, but he just needs to keep trying. After all, skiing has its ups and downs.

STONE ARCH BOOKS
a capstone imprint